Scam

Scam

Lesley Choyce

orca soundings

ORCA BOOK PUBLISHERS

Library and Archives Canada Cataloguing in Publication

Choyce, Lesley, 1951-, author
Scam / Lesley Choyce.
(Orca soundings)

Issued in print and electronic formats.
ISBN 978-1-4598-1174-4 (paperback).—ISBN 978-1-4598-1175-1 (pdf).—
ISBN 978-1-4598-1176-8 (epub)

I. Title. II. Series: Orca soundings
PS8555.H668S23 2016   jc813'.54   c2015-904536-3
                                               c2015-904537-1

First published in the United States, 2016
Library of Congress Control Number: 2015946246

Summary: In this high-interest novel for teen readers,
a boy deals with his mother's death, a move to a group home
and a strange new friend who helps him cope with it all.

*Orca Book Publishers is dedicated to preserving the environment and has
printed this book on Forest Stewardship Council® certified paper.*

Orca Book Publishers gratefully acknowledges the support for its
publishing programs provided by the following agencies: the Government
of Canada through the Canada Book Fund and the Canada Council
for the Arts, and the Province of British Columbia through
the BC Arts Council and the Book Publishing Tax Credit.

Cover image by iStock.com

ORCA BOOK PUBLISHERS
www.orcabook.com

Printed and bound in Canada.

19 18 17 16 • 4 3 2 1

In memory of Jim Lotz—free thinker, activist, mentor, friend and great spirit.

Plenty of them. Looking back, it seems that she could have pulled herself together, but every time she planned to clean up her act, something would surface that would drag her down. She had tried her share of drugs. Mostly different pills. I was never sure which were the worst. Painkillers sometimes. Antidepressants. But it wasn't like she got them from a doctor.

It got worse over the years. I tried to get her to ease off. She tried to quit a few times, but by the time I was sixteen, I guess I knew it wasn't going to stop. It was wrecking her health. I worried about her all the time. I tried to help. I really did. But it didn't do any good.

And then it happened. It was on a Wednesday a week after school was out for the summer. I woke up in our rundown apartment and the sun was shining in. I could hear pigeons out on the window ledges. My mom seemed to be sleeping in, but that wasn't unusual. But by eleven o'clock I went into her room to check on her. I'd had nightmares about this a million times, but they were never as bad as the real thing.

She was gone, and there was no bringing her back. End of story.

Or, in this case, beginning of story.

It's hard for most people to imagine my life. Not many people were as alone in the world as I was. I was trying to "protect" my mom up until then. I was trying to keep her going. I did the cooking. I paid the bills. We had welfare money coming in—not much, but enough to squeak by. When it came time to meet with our social worker, I got her cleaned up. I made us look respectable. Or at least like we were doing okay. I was a good cover-up artist. I knew that if they wanted to, the social workers could have me sent away to a group home. I couldn't let that happen.

Mom went along when I took charge like that. That was my part of "protecting us"—that is, keeping everyone from seeing what basket cases we were. Because of my cover-up, I didn't really have any friends. And there were no relatives who wanted anything to do with us. Aside from social assistance, we were on our own.

But now my mom was gone. I was truly on my own. And it really sucked.

Chapter Two

Picture this.

It's five days after my mom's death. A warm, sunny summer day. But I feel, like, terrible. How can I feel any other way? When my mom died, our social worker, a nice but frazzled woman named Emma, took over. She handled the cremation and organized a funeral. And now I was walking down the street on my way to that funeral service. Emma said it was the right thing to do for my mom. Not that we ever had anything to do with a church. The people who would be there would not be family or friends. They would be members of that church. The minister there did these services for welfare families when someone died.

I hated the idea. I didn't want to go. My mom was dead, and this would be a bunch of strangers trying to do a good deed by showing up for me— Josh Haslett, poor teenage boy who lost his mother to drugs and bad health. Screw them.

I had almost decided not to go to the service at all. It would only make me feel worse. I was trying not to think about my options. Well, I really didn't have much in the way of options. I didn't want to think about my future.

Maybe I had no future outside of being placed in a group home. Screw that.

But then this strange thing happened.

This girl walked up to me out of the blue. "Great day," she says. "I love this weather."

Girls don't usually stop me on the street and strike up a conversation about weather. What was with that? I just stared at her.

"Sorry. Sometimes I freak people out. I was just trying to be friendly."

I didn't know what to say. "Yeah, that's okay. Sorry. I was a little preoccupied."

"I'm Lindsey."

"I'm Josh."

"Short for Joshua?"

"I guess." Nobody had ever called me Joshua that I could recall, except for my mom when I was really young.

"Lindsey is short for Lindsey. The name has something to do with a tree on an island. Scottish, I think."

Why was she telling me this? I wondered. Maybe she was a nutcase. I was thinking of walking away. But I suddenly realized that for the first time since my mom died, I wasn't thinking gloomy thoughts.

"What kind of tree?" I asked, feeling foolish even as I said it.

"I don't know," she said. "I should look it up sometime. I just picture this beautiful, big tree on a small island in the ocean."

She had a big smile now, this cute and friendly nutcase of a girl.

"So?" she asked.

"So what?"

"Where are you going on a beautiful day like this?"

I almost told her, but I held back. "Nowhere in particular."

"Can I walk nowhere in particular with you?"

"If you want," I said, realizing how stupid that sounded. But I think I smiled just then.

"That's good. At first I thought you couldn't smile. I thought maybe you had something wrong with your mouth."

"I don't have anything wrong with my mouth," I said.

"That's good," Lindsey said.

So we walked. And we talked about silly things. And I knew I was going to be late for the funeral, but right then I didn't care.

If you are with me so far, you are thinking, Hey, this is like some really cheesy Hollywood film about a messed-up kid who meets a beautiful girl on the street who changes his life.

Well, it is and it isn't.

After some more walking, and her running commentary about birds, clouds, trees, oceans, faraway places and hairstyles, she suddenly stopped. "I gotta go now," she said. "But I'm hoping we can do this again. Can I give you a hug?"

I smiled but didn't say a thing.

And she wrapped her arms around me and squeezed. It felt really, really good.

And then she grabbed my hand and said my name once—"Joshua." Then she turned and walked away with a bouncy kind of walk.

And so I ended up standing there. Smiling like an idiot.

A few seconds more of feeling stunned and then I took a deep breath and remembered where I was going. I took a few more steps before I realized my wallet was missing.

Chapter Three

I stopped dead in my tracks as it sunk in. That girl had stolen my wallet when she hugged me. What a totally rotten thing to do. I should have known there was something wrong, really wrong, with the way she came on to me. I felt anger welling up inside.

I sat down on a low wall to try to sort out all the weird feelings pulsing through me. Then a voice inside me tried to calm me down. What had I really lost? A wallet with all of five dollars in it and my high school ID. Nothing much at all.

And then I remembered what else. *Damn her*.

I got up and started running in the direction I had come from. If it took all day, I would find her.

At first I thought there would be no way for me to track her down, but it turned out she wasn't far from where we had met. I found her as she was walking out of a corner store. She saw me running toward her and turned to go back into the store.

I went in and confronted her. "Why did you do that?" I snarled, having a hard time catching my breath.

"Do what?" she asked.

The guy behind the counter was looking at us now. "Hey. Take it outside."

Lindsey walked back outside, and I followed her. I half expected her to run, but she didn't. She stopped on the sidewalk and looked me directly in the eyes.

"You stole my wallet," I insisted.

Then she did a strange thing. She smiled. "You mean this?" she said, holding it up.

I grabbed it from her. "How could you do that?"

"Sorry, it's what I do."

I flipped it open and pulled out a five-dollar bill. "I only had five dollars."

"I know," she said. "Poor you."

"Yeah, poor me. But I don't care about the money."

"What do you care about?"

I didn't want to show her at first, but then I realized I needed to tell her what she had stolen from me. I wanted to show her how nasty her actions were. I fumbled with the wallet, lifted a leather flap and pulled out the crinkled, yellowed photograph. "My mom," I said. "This is the only picture of my mom that I own."

"You must really like your mom," she said, still acting like this was all a joke.

"Screw you. My mom's dead. She only died a few days ago." Just saying those words made the pain of her loss much more real, much more awful.

Everything about Lindsey changed then. She looked down at the sidewalk. Then she looked up at me. "You're not joking, are you?"

"It's no joke. I was on my way to her funeral service at a church I've never set foot in before."

"No way."

"I didn't want to go. I don't want to be there. But I was trying. I thought it was the right thing to do."

"Then you need to be there. Look, I'm so sorry I did that to you. I wouldn't have if I knew what was going on."

"But why would you do it to anyone?"

She looked away. "I could explain. But not now. Look, you need to go to that church."

I felt crappy. "I'm not going. Not now."

"You have to go."

I wanted to smack this girl. I really did. It wasn't just her. It was the whole rotten mess I was in. I must have been holding my breath, because I suddenly let out a big sigh. "Forget it," I said. "Just forget it." And I started to walk away. Lindsey just stood there.

I was maybe ten feet away when she ran up from behind. "Josh," she said. "You're going to that funeral. And I'm going with you."

Chapter Four

"I've never been to a funeral before," I told her as we walked.

"Neither have I," she said, but I wasn't sure she was telling me the truth. "We're like funeral virgins."

I scowled at her.

"Sorry," she said. "I'll get serious."

We were late for the service. There were maybe twenty people in the church pews. I didn't recognize anyone except for my social worker, Emma. She noticed me coming in, walked back and led us to seats near the front as people sang a slow, sad song.

Lindsey sat down beside me on the empty wooden bench. The song ended and the minister began to read from the bible. My mom had never been religious. We'd never once gone to church, so this seemed very odd, very wrong. For a second I considered getting up and walking out of there. Or running.

Lindsey must have noticed me getting antsy, because first she touched my leg and then she took my hand and held it. Who was this nut job of a girl anyway? But then I closed my eyes as the minister droned on, and all I could think about was the fact that I was glad I was not alone.

I don't remember much else about the service. There was no coffin. My mom had been cremated. The minister spoke about Jesus and about resurrection and about how my mom's spirit was there in the church but that she had also "gone home." If my mom had been here, really here, she would have hated it all. As the service was coming to a close, people stood up and sang another song from the hymn book. I had been fighting my emotions through the whole thing, but suddenly I found myself crying.

We sat there, Lindsey and me, while everyone else was standing. She put her arm around me. And I cried. I hadn't cried in a long time. Not even when I had found my mom dead in her bed. But now I let it out.

I sobbed, and my body shook. And Lindsey held on to me and didn't let go.

People nodded to us as they left the church. The minister came over and said something that was supposed to be comforting, I guess, but I wasn't really listening to the words.

As we got up to go, the social worker came up and introduced herself to Lindsey.

"You gonna be okay?" she asked me. "Do you want me to come over and be with you?"

"No," I said. "My uncle is coming in from out of town to stay with me for a few days."

"That's good," Emma said. "I was afraid you were all alone. I'll be over to sort things out with you in a couple of days, okay?"

"Sure," I said. I had no uncle—not one that would ever come over to help out anyway.

As we walked away from the church, the world seemed different to me. I don't know how to explain it. Just different. Unreal, I guess.

"Josh, are you going be all right?" Lindsey asked. I think she asked me three times before I heard her.

"I don't know," I finally answered. "I've been worrying about my mom for so long. That's what I did. Every day. And I tried to help. And sometimes it seemed like things were going to be okay. But now she's gone."

Lindsey looked at me and touched my face. "It's not your fault."

"Yeah, I think it is. I should have taken better care of her."

"I'm so sorry. You must have really loved her."

I took a deep breath. My head was still filled with fog. That damn church service didn't do me much good. It certainly didn't do my mother any good. And then there was this girl beside me. Who was she? Why was she walking with me? I took a deep breath. I tried to focus on something.

I was afraid to think about returning to that crappy apartment alone. I was afraid of what my life was going to be like tonight and tomorrow and the day after that. I was afraid, and I was alone in the world. All I knew right now was that I wanted this crazy girl, this Lindsey, to stay beside me, to keep talking.

"What about *your* parents?" I asked. "Tell me about them."

"My mom and dad are the world's most invisible parents. In some ways, they are every teenager's dream. My dad works about sixty hours a week, and my mom has all this social stuff on the go. They are probably okay people. They're just hardly ever home. There's food in the fridge. They even gave my brother and me a credit card we can use for clothes and stuff. They trust us. Which, believe me, is totally nuts."

"You have a brother?"

"Yeah. Caleb. He was raised by video games and YouTube videos."

"Is he like you?"

"You mean, is he a thief?"

"No. I don't know. What is he like?"

"Well, he has his problems."

"Like what?" Suddenly I was interested in other people's problems. Anything to get my mind off my own.

"Well, he gets depressed easily. But he's also very insecure. So he acts out. He does things to try to impress people. He thinks if he can draw attention to himself, people will like him."

"Like what?"

"Well, in the last year he has started to think he's a great graffiti artist. He goes by the name Yo-Yo."

"Yo-Yo?"

"I think it has to do with the depression thing. He says that he gets down, but he always bounces back. Yo-Yo."

"I've seen it. I've seen that name. Big puffy letters in the weirdest places."

"That's my brother. If he can get at it, he'll try to tag it."

"But why?"

Lindsey threw up her hands. "You'd have to ask Caleb. Caleb the Conqueror, he used to call himself when he was in his superhero phase. He's been caught more than once. He's not that careful. But, like he says, he always bounces back. That's the Yo-Yo for you."

We were standing outside my apartment building—a dirty three-story brick building with trash on the front steps. "I'm home."

"Now what?"

"I don't know. I walk in there and try to figure out where my life goes from here."

"What about me?" Lindsey asked.

"What about you?"

"Well, we did this funeral thing together, right?"

"Yeah. Well, you stole my wallet first, and then we did the funeral thing."

"I know. But I didn't know your mom had just died. Besides, it wasn't personal."

"It seemed pretty personal at the time."

"I can explain, but maybe not now. Now I want you to tell me that we can be friends. We had a bad start, but it's getting better, right?"

"It's hard for me to think about anything getting better," I said. And I almost turned and began to go up those trashy steps. But, despite all the weirdness, I knew that Lindsey was some kind of lifeline for me.

"Yeah, if you want to be my friend, I'd like that," I said.

Lindsey smiled then. It was a great smile. "Hold out your hand."

I held out my hand, and she wrote something on it. An email address.

"I have to go to the library if I want to check emails."

"Okay." She flipped my hand over and wrote a phone number on it. "You got a phone?"

"I have my mom's cell phone. It's really old. Guess it's mine now."

"Call me?"

I tried smiling back, but it was like my face wasn't working. I started up the steps, then turned and said, "Thanks. Thanks, Lindsey."

Chapter Five

I spent the next day alone in the apartment. I kept thinking my mom was going to walk in the door and everything would be okay, but I knew that wasn't going to happen. I was in a dark and lonely place. I found my mom's old cell phone and plugged it in so the battery wouldn't go dead. It seemed to take an enormous amount of energy to do just that, to plug the damn thing in the wall. I copied Lindsey's phone number onto three different pieces of paper. I placed one on the kitchen table and one on the table by my bed, and I put one in my wallet.

But I didn't call her.

I slept a lot. The more I slept, the more tired I felt.

And then the buzzer rang. I looked out and could see it was Emma, and she had a guy with her. I hit the door buzzer to let them in. What else could I do?

"Hi, Josh. How are you doing?" she asked.

"I'm okay, I guess."

"Your uncle here?"

"He's out."

"Okay. This is Darren," she said, nodding to the guy beside her.

"Hi, Josh," he said. "Good to meet you. Sorry about your loss." Darren looked to be about thirty. He had longish hair and seemed to be a nice guy.

"Yeah. Me too."

"Darren runs a group home over on Cumberland," Emma said. "You know much about group homes?"

I shook my head no.

"It's not like the old days," Darren said. "Ours is small. Right now we only have four other kids there. We think you'll fit in."

I looked at Emma. I'd never really trusted her, but she'd always been straight with my mom and me, always tried to help out, even when my mom pushed her away. I think she knew there was no uncle in the picture, but she didn't come right out and say it.

"I gotta do this?" I asked her.

"Josh, you're sixteen. We can't let you stay here by yourself. Maybe in a year or two you'll be okay on your own. But for now, you need to let us help you."

Darren handed me a card. "This is the address. It's not that far from here.

We'd like it if you could walk over later today. On your own. Just come check us out. I'll introduce you to the other guys. I'm not gonna say we're like one big happy family. In fact, we are one weird little family or maybe not family at all. But we're in it together. I live there too. This is my life. This is what I do. Just give us a chance."

I looked at Emma. "What about this apartment? What happens to my mom's stuff?"

"For now," she said, "nothing. Everything will be here. We'll continue to pay the rent until things settle down. You can come back here to visit in the days, if you like."

Darren was playing cheerleader. He smiled and gave me two thumbs-up. Then they turned to go. "Hope to see you later today," Darren said.

That afternoon I left the apartment for the first time since the funeral service. The sunlight was brighter—too bright. The street sounds seemed louder. Everything felt different—unfamiliar, like I'd never even been here before.

I walked to Cumberland Street and found the house—just a nondescript suburban house on a quiet dead-end street. I rang the doorbell, and a fat kid came to the door. "Who are you?" he asked.

"Josh," I said.

"You selling something?"

"No. I'm here to see Darren."

He rolled his eyes. "Oh shit," he said and then yelled, "Darren, the new kid is here."

Darren bounded to the door with a big grin on his face. He shook my hand, and the fat kid wandered off inside. "That's Kyle," he said. "We're working on his social skills. C'mon in."

The first thing that struck me about the house was that everything was completely ordinary. There was a living room with a TV, a kitchen and a few small bedrooms. "Don't blame me for the home decorating," Darren said. "It was like this when I got here. Do you think you can handle it?"

"Handle what?"

"Think you can live in a place like this?"

I shrugged.

"Josh," Darren said, "you've had a big loss. If I was in your shoes, I'd be a mess. I never lost a parent. We just want to give you a place that is safe and give you a chance to recover. Aside from Kyle, you'll have three other kids to share the house with. And me. I'm supposedly in charge." He opened a door to one of the bedrooms. "You'll bunk in here with Noah."

Noah was lying on one of the two beds in the room. He had dark hair, wore glasses and was reading a book. He looked up at me and nodded and said, "Like the guy with the ark. Only I don't have any animals. We're not allowed to have pets."

I nodded uncertainly.

"Welcome aboard," he said. "But I might as well tell you outright. I fart a lot, so you'll have to get used to it."

"Thanks for the heads-up," I said. I set my backpack down on the empty bed and let Darren lead me downstairs to what he called the family room.

"Noah had the crap beat out of him by his father on a regular basis. It's not the farts you need to worry about. He wakes up screaming sometimes. Think you'll be all right with that?"

"I dunno. I guess so. What should I do when that happens?"

Darren smiled at me. "Do what you'd want someone else to do if you woke up screaming. You'll figure it out."

There were two guys in the family room about my age. Darren nodded to them. "Connor and Brian, this is Josh."

Connor looked me over. I could tell he was one of those kids who liked to size a person up and stick a label on them. He held up his hand and said, "Welcome, loser number five," as if he was a host on some game show. "Can we have a round of applause for Josh." This didn't seem funny to me at all. The other kid, Brian, didn't say anything. He had some kind of handheld video game that he went on playing.

Darren led me back into the kitchen and opened the fridge. "Here's the heart of this place. What's here is yours as much as everyone else's. We all gotta share, and I hope you'll chip in with some chores. For now, that's it. Make yourself at home. What would you like to do first?"

What I wanted to do was get out of there and go back home, but I was playing it cool. "Okay if I just go for a walk?"

"Absolutely. Dinner's at five. Connor's making macaroni with chunks of hot dogs cut up in it. It's his specialty."

"I wouldn't want to miss that," I said.

As I walked out of there, I felt a new wave of sadness sweep over me. The loss of my mom was still sinking in. We'd never been much of a family. But it was my life as I knew it. I loved her, and in her own way she loved me. I would never get that back. I'd never get her back. If I'd thought I could run, I would have. But I didn't have any place to run to.

Chapter Six

The girl. All I could think about was calling Lindsey.

I found my way to a park and sat on a bench. Pigeons flew down and started marching around in front of me. I guess they thought I was going to feed them, but I had nothing. I took out my wallet. The five-dollar bill was still there. So was the faded picture of my mom.

For a split second, I was ready to burst into tears. But I pushed that back. Instead, I unfolded the little scrap of paper with Lindsey's phone number on it.

I punched in the numbers on my mom's old cell phone. It rang. What was I going to say to her?

"Hello?"

"Lindsey?"

"Yeah. Who's this?"

"Josh."

"Josh. This is weird. No one actually calls me to talk on my cell."

"I don't think I can text from this phone."

"That's okay. It's good to hear from you. How are you doing?"

"I'm hanging in there," I said. "What are you doing?"

"Nothing. I'm bored out of my gourd."

"Can we do something together?" I couldn't believe I was asking her this.

I wasn't even sure I trusted this girl. Maybe she was playing some freaking game by being nice to me.

"Sure. Like what?"

"I don't know."

"Where are you?" she asked.

"I'm not far from where we met."

"Okay. I'll come meet you there. Same corner where I first saw you. I'm leaving the house now." And she hung up.

I almost didn't recognize her when I saw her twenty minutes later. She had on an old flannel shirt and dirty ripped jeans and men's work boots. Her hair was kind of stringy, and she was wearing a Boston Red Sox ballcap.

She walked up to me and gave me a hug. I think I pulled back a little, remembering what happened the last time. But I tried to relax. Her body felt good against me.

"How do you like the way I look?"

"I don't know. You look okay, but I almost didn't recognize you."

"It's all part of the game."

"What game?" I asked.

"Look around. Can you tell which people on the street are tourists?"

I looked around. "No. How could I tell?"

"Check it out," she said. "That guy there with the Disneyland T-shirt and the expensive backpack. And his wife in the sunglasses. Tourists for sure."

"Why does it matter?"

"Watch."

So I watched as she walked toward them and said something. They stopped. She talked for a bit, and then it looked like maybe she was about to cry.

That's when the woman opened her purse and took out a wallet. I was freaking out, thinking Lindsey was about to grab it and run. But it wasn't like that. The man stood there frowning, but the wife handed over a bill. Lindsey must have kept talking, because then the woman handed over a second bill. And a third. Lindsey bent over and kissed her hand and then turned, looked straight at me and flashed the money.

When she came back, she grabbed my arm and ushered me down a side street, a big grin on her face. "Like taking candy from a baby. Look. Twenty bucks."

"What did you say to them?"

"I told them I was living on the street and was sick of it. I wanted to go home and needed money for bus fare."

"But that was a total scam."

"Totally." She was smiling. I guess I was frowning.

"Josh. Lighten up. I'll admit it wasn't my most creative moment, but I can do better."

"No. It's not that. It's just that you lied and cheated those people out of their money."

"Relax, preacher boy. It's just a game. I'm not hurting anyone. Think of it like acting. I'm a good actor, right?"

"You're a good scam artist."

"I don't like that term," she said and looked hurt. Then angry. "Hey, do you want to hang out with me, or should I just go home and leave you alone?"

I hung my head. No, I didn't want to be alone. And I could see I had pissed her off.

"This is who I am," she said. "So get over it."

I tried a fake smile.

"That's better. Now let's go get a coffee and something to eat. My treat."

Chapter Seven

At the coffee shop, we sat by the window. Lindsey bought us each a fancy coffee drink. It tasted like nothing I'd ever had before. "Cappuccino," she said. "My favorite."

"What if that tourist couple came in and saw you sitting here with me, drinking cappuccino?"

Lindsey shrugged. "Hey, homeless people need to live a little once in a while, I'd tell them."

"How come you didn't just ask *me* for money the other day? Why did you steal my wallet?"

"Well, you looked like an easy target at first, and I was gonna do the sob-story routine, but I realized I wasn't dressed for it. And then, as I was talking to you, I thought you were kind of cute. So I gave you a hug."

"And then stole my wallet."

"I call it lifting. I lifted your wallet. I guess I got carried away, and I wanted to see if I could get away with it."

I looked down at my cappuccino. I was thinking that this girl was trouble. Why was I hanging out with her?

"I see that look on your face," she said.

"Why do you do it?"

"I told you. It's a game. It's a challenge. I try out new techniques. New angles. I like the buzz I get from doing it."

"What if you get caught? What if you get in trouble with the police?"

"I haven't so far. Besides, it's all part of the challenge. The trick is to get away with it."

"I suppose you like to shoplift too?"

Lindsey laughed. "I used to. But that was too easy. If I got caught, I could always talk my way out of it. But enough about me. What about you? Tell me what you do for fun." But as soon as she said it, a curious look came over her face. I think she realized, knowing what I had been through, that I wasn't having much fun these days.

I told her about the group home, about Darren and about the four guys I had met.

"I guess there's not much fun there," she said. "How are you gonna live in a place like that?"

"I don't know," I admitted.

And then she surprised me again, this girl who liked to rip people off and scam anyone and do anything she thought she could get away with. She said, "What can I do to help?"

I swallowed my drink and thought about it. Aside from being here with Lindsey, I had to admit to myself, I really didn't have anything good in my life. And I did like being with her. "Be my friend," I finally said.

"Girlfriend?" she asked, shocking me.

"Maybe."

She smiled again. "I don't seem to have much luck with guys. Or maybe, to put it another way, they don't have much luck with me."

I almost laughed. I was imagining the kind of games she could play with a guy. How could you ever know if she was sincere or just role playing? "I guess they get pissed off when you steal their wallets."

"Shush," she said. "No. Usually, I just lose interest when I realize how shallow they are. And they all seem to be shallow. Are you?"

"Am I what?"

"Shallow. Superficial. Trivial. Small-minded. One-dimensional."

"Look," I said. "I don't even know. Maybe I'm like all the rest. But I've spent most of my life just trying to hold my mom and me together. It was mostly about survival and working the system—the social workers—so that my mom wouldn't go to jail and I wouldn't be sent away. I didn't have any time to be shallow. Or trivial."

"When you say *work the system*, what do you mean?"

"You know, say what the social workers wanted to hear. Tell them my mom had no problems, that everything was okay, that she wasn't spending welfare money on drugs. You know?"

"No, I don't know. But it sounds like you had to lie to them."

"I did what I had to do."

"So in your own way, you are not that different from me."

"What do you mean?"

"You learned to be a scam artist of sorts. You had to be creative. You had to lie. You had to play the game, and you learned to play it well."

"I never thought of it as a game. It was serious."

"Okay, but now I see another side of you. I can work with that."

"What do you mean?"

"I can teach you things. We can do some stuff together. Take it up to the next level."

I didn't know what she meant or how to respond, so I just kept my mouth shut, sat there and stared at her.

Chapter Eight

Lindsey made me promise to meet her back at the coffee shop the next day at one in the afternoon. "I'm going to have on a different outfit. So I want you to dress up. Wear something nice. Something formal, if you have it." She kissed me on the cheek when she left.

I headed back to the group home with a weird mix of emotions sweeping through me. The loss of my mom. The new living situation. This girl, who I really liked but might never know if she was telling me the truth or just being a good actor. And why had she told me to wear something nice, something formal?

On my way back to the group home, I noticed all the graffiti on an overpass and more nearby on a school wall. Most prominent was *Yo-Yo*. I'd seen it before, but now there was a connection. Lindsey's brother Caleb was doing this—tagging in big bold letters, in some really difficult locations. What the hell did he do? Use ladders, hang over the side by a rope? I wondered why on earth anyone would take chances just to scrawl his nickname on a bridge or wall. But then, I guessed Caleb and Lindsey had grown up in one crazy little family.

I hung out in my room for a while and tried to get to know Noah. He was still lying on his bed, reading a science-fiction novel that must have had five hundred pages. "You like to read, huh?" I said, trying to strike up a conversation.

"Takes my mind off things," he said and then added, "Sorry about your mom."

"Yeah," I said.

"My mom left when I was little. She got tired of being beat up by my dad."

"Ouch."

"So he took it out on me."

"What was he so angry about?"

"I never figured it out."

"How'd you end up here?" I asked.

"He nearly killed me."

"My father left a long time ago. I hardly remember him."

"Man, are you lucky," Noah said. "I wish my father had left."

"How do you like living here?"

"It's okay, really. No one hits me. Connor is a pain in the ass, but Darren keeps a lid on things. Brian's the only genuine criminal in the house, but he's really okay once you get to know him."

"What did he do?"

"Tried to burn down his school. Aside from that, he seems pretty normal."

Despite the fact that Noah seemed like he was hurting, I thought he might not be so bad as a roommate. I sized him up and realized he was about the same height and weight as me. "Noah," I asked, "do you have any nice clothes I could borrow? Just for tomorrow."

"What do you mean, *nice*?"

"I don't know. Like formal."

He got off his bed and opened the closet. He held out a white shirt, a tie and dress pants. "I've got some shiny shoes in here somewhere," he said, rooting around the bottom of the closet. "You're welcome to them, if you want. I never have a reason to wear them."

"Thanks, man," I said. "I really appreciate it."

"No problem," he said. He never asked me what I wanted them for.

Dinner was that Connor special Darren had mentioned. It wasn't great, but I hadn't eaten much since my mom had died, so I ate like a pig. "The new boy has an appetite," Connor said in a smart-ass way. "He shovels more in his face than Kyle does."

Kyle gave him the finger and snarled. Noah looked at me and smiled. I couldn't quite figure out Brian. He just looked at his food and ate slowly.

"I'm going to work on you guys," Darren said. "Turn you all into vegetarians. Wait and see."

"Frig off," Connor said, but he said it in such a way that we all laughed, even Brian.

"Healthy body, healthy mind," Darren said.

"Sick body, sick mind, is more like it," Connor chimed in. "How come I'm not getting a bit more appreciation for my cuisine?"

Truth was, the hot dogs and macaroni slathered with ketchup tasted good.

"Sorry, Connor," Darren said. "I can tell that you made this meal with love."

"Hey, at least I didn't spit in it."

"We all thank you for that," Darren said and laughed.

It was clear that Darren got along with the guys. He had a light touch.

After dinner I sat down outside on the steps as the sun was setting. Darren came out and sat down beside me. "So far?"

"So far, okay."

"We need to come up with a plan for you."

"What kind of plan?"

"I don't know how long you'll be here. Could be a while. But then, in the not-too-distant future, you're gonna be out there. And your fate will be your decision."

"So far, nothing in my life seems to have been my decision."

"Feel like a victim?"

"You bet I do."

"What if I said there are no victims?"

"Then I'd say bullshit."

"I mean, if you feel like a victim, you stay that way. If you take charge, no matter how hard it is, then you control your future."

"Sounds good on paper," I said. "Not sure it will work for me."

"Just think about it. Anyway, I'm glad you're here with us. Be brave. Trust me, there will be some rocky moments."

"Like dinner?"

"Dinner was nothing. That was easy."

"Will Brian try to burn the place down?" I asked.

"I don't think so. He likes us. And besides, we hide the matches."

Chapter Nine

That night I dreamed I was back living with my mom and everything was okay. Or, at least, as okay as it ever was while she was alive. It seemed like everything that had happened in the last week was a dream and not real at all. Then things kind of got jumbled up as to what was real and what wasn't—until Noah started shouting in his sleep. That woke me up. And at first I was more confused than ever.

"No! Don't! I didn't do it!" Noah yelled.

I shook myself awake and sat up, realizing where I was and being suddenly reminded of my mom's death. The room was dark, but there was light coming in from the hallway.

"No! Please!" Noah pleaded, still in some kind of nightmare. My guess was that he was reliving scenes with his father. I didn't know if I should wake him or not. What was the right thing to do?

Darren appeared in the doorway with a flashlight. He saw me sitting up in my bed.

"Sorry about this, Josh. I warned you that Noah does this sometimes."

"What do you do?"

Darren sighed. "Sometimes I do nothing and wait for the dream to go away. If it's really bad, I sit beside him and try to gently wake him up."

Darren sat down in a chair by Noah, and we sat in silence for a minute. Noah seemed to settle back down, and soon he was snoring. Darren looked at me and laughed quietly. "Dreams are a way of processing some of the bad stuff in your life. Noah had it pretty rough. He's still working through it. What about you? Having any bad dreams?"

For some reason I didn't want to get into it. "Nah," I said. "I'm okay."

"Good," he said. "Just remember, you've had a major loss. You have to let it out somewhere. Otherwise, you explode. You're gonna feel bad and feel sorry for yourself for a long time, but you also have to face the world."

I was beginning to see that this was Darren's way. He played his role like an older brother, one with lots of advice to dole out. But I didn't mind.

Noah continued to snore. Darren said, "Good night," and left.

I tried to get back to sleep, but I couldn't help thinking about where I was and what came next. How was I going to make it through the summer? What would it be like to go back to school? How long might I have to stay here in this group home? Even worse, where would I would go after that? I felt like I simply wasn't ready to deal with anything.

So I tried to stop thinking about it all. And then an image of Lindsey floated into my head. The old me would have been scared of a girl like that. A bad girl. A tease. A liar and a scammer. Who knew what else? But I had to admit I looked forward to seeing her the next day. Saturday. And she'd asked me to dress up. What was that about? Was this some kind of real date?

Noah slept quietly for the rest of the night. In the morning, Darren walked the halls and announced, "Rise and shine, campers. You don't want to miss this one. This is the first day of the rest of your life." I could see that Mr. Sunshine could get on your nerves after a while. But as I stumbled into the kitchen and saw him scrambling eggs and frying bacon, I decided I could forgive him for his annoying cheerfulness, and apparently the others did too. We all ate like we hadn't seen any food in a month. Even Noah, who seemed to have survived his nightmares.

Darren had a little garden in the backyard, but he was the only one who worked on it that morning. I wasn't in the mood for any more of his advice, so I stayed clear of him. When the afternoon rolled around, I tried on Noah's pants and shirt and shoes. The shoes were a bit tight, but the rest seemed to fit. I looked in the mirror and Noah watched as I tried to tie the tie but failed miserably. I didn't think I had ever worn a tie. Finally, Noah helped me out. "Where are you going, anyway?"

"I don't really know."

"But there's a girl involved, right?"

"Yeah."

"Lucky you," he said, offering me some kind of gel to put in my hair.

"Yeah, lucky me."

I met up with Lindsey as planned, in the coffee shop of the new downtown library. She saw me walking toward her and stood up. She had on a dress and makeup and carried a large, expensive-looking handbag. She looked beautiful. I suddenly felt nervous and not at all like myself in my new look.

"You clean up real nice," she said in a fake Southern accent.

"So do you," I said. As we stood there sizing each other up, I noticed that some adults were looking at us and smiling. The perfect young couple. Ha.

"Now what?" I asked.

Lindsey checked her watch. "At two o'clock we're going to go somewhere."

"Where?"

"To a wedding," she said, giving me a mysterious smile. "Well, we'll go to the wedding at the church, and then we won't look out of place when we get to the wedding party."

"Friends of yours?"

"Not really."

"What's this all about?"

"What, you don't like weddings?"

"I've never been to one."

"You have a long list of things you've never done?" she asked and gave me a funny look.

That was just like Lindsey, to put it that way. It made me feel even more embarrassed.

So for the second time in less than a week, the second time in my life, I found myself sitting in a church. With a pretty girl. The service was like something out of a movie. People smiling, crying, a young couple walking down an aisle strewn with rose petals. The whole thing had nothing to do with the world I had come from. It was like I had landed on another planet.

When it was over, we followed the other people outside. "And now for the good part," Lindsey said. As the couple was being photographed, we walked with the others to a nearby church hall. Inside, people milled around and chatted with each other. Lindsey held my arm and walked me into the center of the room. Three separate bars were set up, and people were getting drinks.

Lindsey walked over to the closest one and asked for two glasses of wine. The man behind the bar didn't question her, but he did give me a wink as he handed her the glasses.

"Isn't this great?" she said, giving me one of the glasses and taking a sip.

"Another first," I said as I sipped the wine. I'd had beer before and even sneaked some whiskey once, but I'd never had wine. Lindsey drained her glass quickly, and, like a fool, I did the same. She went back for seconds.

Lindsey led me on a tour around the hall and stopped in front of a table piled with gifts and envelopes for the newlyweds. "Must be nice," she said, pointing at the wedding booty.

Suddenly it struck me as very odd that we were part of this scene. "What are we doing here anyway?" I asked.

She didn't answer my question. "Aren't you having fun?"

I could feel the wine doing funny things to my head. "I guess so."

"Just relax and enjoy the party."

We wandered around the room some more. I followed Lindsey's lead, nodding and smiling at the people we encountered. No one asked us who we were or why we were here.

And then the bride and groom entered the hall. All eyes were on them. That's when Lindsey grabbed me by my sleeve and led me back toward that table with the gifts. As everyone oohed and aahed at the wedding couple, Lindsey began picking up envelopes from the gift table and stashing them in her over-sized purse.

I couldn't believe it. "What are you doing?" I whispered.

"Be quiet," she hissed as she grabbed another handful of envelopes and started walking casually to the door. Everyone was still making a fuss over the newly married couple, who looked like they had just stepped out of a magazine.

As I followed Lindsey out into the sunlight, I was both shocked and angry. "That was a truly rotten thing to do."

"Just shut up and keep walking."

I thought about getting the hell away from her. I felt like I had been tricked into being part of this, her worst scam yet. "You've done this before?" I asked, the anger rising further in me.

"No. First time," she said nonchalantly.

"Why?"

She stopped in her tracks. "Get over it," she said. "This is what I do. It's my life, so don't go judging me. It's who I am. Take it or leave it."

We walked for ten minutes in complete silence. Lindsey stopped and sat down on a park bench by a wire trashcan. I sat down beside her. At first I just looked away. But then I turned toward her. I watched as she opened the first envelope, found a check inside and threw it and the card in the trashcan. The same thing happened with two more envelopes. Then she opened the next envelope and found two fifty-dollar bills. "Bingo," she said. "At least some people still give cash. Here. Open a couple of these."

She tossed three envelopes in my lap, but I just stared at them.

"Go on. Do it."

It's hard to explain why I didn't bail on her right then. I was really pissed off. I didn't want any part of this. But then I remembered that this was the girl who had sat beside me through my mother's funeral. I opened my first envelope and read the inscription inside:

May your lives be filled with love and happiness.

Love,
Brett and Sybil

And there was a hundred-dollar bill. Lindsey looked over, gave me a big goofy smile, took the hundred and stashed it in my shirt pocket and then threw the card into the trashcan. I handed the other envelopes back to her, tilted my head back and closed my eyes.

Lindsey continued on like a kid on Christmas morning. When she had opened all the stolen envelopes, she announced, "Five hundred dollars. Not bad. Too bad we can't use those checks."

"Now what?" I asked, feeling totally defeated.

Lindsey tucked another $150 in my shirt pocket. "Even split," she said. "Enough fun for today. This week we go on a spending spree though. I gotta go now." She stood up, leaned over me and kissed me full on the lips. "Thanks for being such a good sidekick." And she walked away.

Chapter Ten

I couldn't sleep that night. I couldn't believe what I had allowed Lindsey to get me into. I'd never stolen anything in my life. Even my mother, hooked on drugs, hadn't stolen. She'd sometimes spent welfare money on street drugs and we didn't have enough to eat, but she hadn't stolen.

Noah couldn't sleep either. I could tell by his breathing. So there we were, lying on beds on either side of the room, wide awake.

"Noah," I asked. "Can I run something past you?"

"Sure." He sat up and turned on a lamp.

So I told him about my day.

"Man," he said. "You didn't strike me as the criminal type."

"That's just it. I'm not. It was her idea."

"But you went along."

"I didn't know what I was getting myself into."

"But if you got caught…"

"I know. So what do you think?"

"You want my opinion?"

"Yes."

"Well," he began slowly. "Is she cute? The girl?"

"Yeah. She's hot."

"How come she chose you?"

I explained how we met.

"That is one crazy chick," Noah said. "She sounds really…interesting."

"Interesting but dangerous."

His eyes were wide now. "What was it you wanted my advice about?"

"I'm not sure I want any more grief in my life than I already have. Should I see her again or just walk away from it?"

Noah looked at me like I had two heads. "Josh, are you out of your mind? If I had a girl like that, I'd rob a bank if she asked me to. What is there to think about?"

I nodded. "Okay. Thanks. Would you mind not mentioning this to anyone else?"

"Secret's safe with me. But I want to hear what happens in the next chapter."

And that was pretty much the end of the conversation. He turned off the light. I eventually drifted off to sleep.

The next day Darren drove us out of town to a trail in a forest. We hiked for two hours. It had been a long, long time since I'd been in the woods, and it felt good. Kyle complained a lot until Connor told him to shut up and threatened to hit him.

"Back off, Connor," Darren said.

"Fat kids don't belong on hikes," Connor said. "Fat kids don't belong anywhere."

Kyle looked humiliated, but Brian came to his defense. "Connor, you have your head so far up your ass, how do you know anything about who belongs where?"

Strangely, Darren didn't say anything, and that seemed to be the end of it. The trail was steep, and I was feeling it in the backs of my calves. The pain felt good. Really good. Noah was right beside me, and we were breathing hard. But not as hard as Kyle. When Connor, Brian and

71

Darren rounded a big rock and were out of sight, we both gave Kyle a hand, helping him up the incline. We were all sweating at that point. That felt good too.

When we stopped for a break on a high ledge overlooking a valley with a lake at the bottom, Darren handed around sandwiches. I was hungry, and they tasted great. I had a flashback to when I was little, and how my mom used to make me liverwurst sandwiches. It was weird, because in the flashback my mom was a good mom. She would wake me up, make me breakfast and help me get ready for school. It was a long time ago, though, and I couldn't tell if it was a real memory or just something I imagined.

When I finished my sandwich, I walked away from the others to take a pee over the ledge. I took out my cell phone and thought about calling Lindsey but discovered there was no signal.

The hike back down was almost as difficult as going up the hill had been. Noah and I hung back and kept an eye on Kyle. Darren knew what we were doing and gave us a thumbs-up but didn't say anything. He wasn't giving any lectures today, but he knew what he was doing. The hike, I think, was good for all of us. It was a challenge, and we did it as a group. As a family, Darren might have said. A weird little family.

That night the house was quiet. I had plugged my cell phone in and left it on. It rang at about two in the morning. It was Lindsey.

"Where were you today?" she asked.

"We went for a hike. In the woods. Sorry I didn't call."

"Are you mad at me?"

I didn't quite know what I was feeling about her, but I remembered what Noah had said. "No," I said. "How can I be mad at you?"

"Can we do something tomorrow?"

"I guess. What did you have in mind?" I was worried about what she might have in mind. What kind of scam would she come up with next?

"Nothing, really. Let's just hang out together. Do something…normal. Maybe go to the park."

"The park sounds good."

"When I see you, I'm going to give you a really big hug."

I fell back asleep, dreaming of Lindsey. Dreaming of Lindsey and me, hand in hand like some kind of dream couple.

Lindsey's idea of normal was finding a quiet spot near the duck pond at Sullivan's Cove and smoking some weed. I didn't want to, so I pretended to smoke but didn't inhale (as the politicians say). Lindsey got kind of dreamy-eyed and laughed a lot and kept commenting on how cute the ducks were.

I asked her about her family and growing up, but she didn't want to talk about it. Then I asked her how she'd gotten into this scamming thing, and she grew much more animated.

"Well, I always liked to pretend things. Just kid stuff. But when I was about twelve, I was really bored. I was walking home from school one day. I stopped this lady and asked if I could use her cell phone to call home. She said yes. I made a fake call home and pretended I only got message. *Mom*, I said, *it's me. I lost my wallet and my phone and don't have any money to catch the bus home. I don't know what to do*. And then I hung up. The lady looked at me and asked how much I needed. I told her that five dollars should do it. She handed me the five, and I started to shake and look worried. She asked me what was wrong. I said I wasn't sure I'd make my bus connection on time and that I might get stuck downtown. I said I was scared to be there on my own. She ended up giving me twenty dollars and told me to take a taxi. She tried to stop one for me, but I said I'd be okay."

"That was the beginning?"

"Yep. I started coming up with inventive strategies after that."

"Like what?"

"Boy, you want to know all the tricks of the trade."

She was giggling a bit now and leaning toward me in a flirty way. She ran her fingers through my hair, and I began to wonder if she was just acting with me as well. She could probably get any guy to believe what she wanted him to believe. I remembered Noah's words about robbing a bank.

"Well," she said, "I picked up some flyers from an animal rights group, and I went to the university. I had a clip-board, and I made up a fake petition. I stopped people and showed them photos of animals used for medical testing. I got them to sign the petition and asked for a donation to the organization. I was very convincing."

"Let me guess. You kept the money."

She smiled and dipped her head. "I guess that's bad, huh?"

"Some people would say so."

"Do you think I'm awful?" she asked.

I shook my head. "No," I said. "I think you're great. You're a little warped though."

"Are you okay with that?"

I smiled and decided to push my own limits. I leaned into her and gave her a kiss.

Chapter Eleven

The more time we spent together, the more I tried to change her.

"I'm addicted," she admitted finally. "I'd miss the challenge and the buzz I get from the game. Let's do another wedding."

"No way."

"What did you do with your money?" she asked. "The money we split from that wedding party?"

I hadn't done anything with it. I'd hidden it in my room. I was saving it for an emergency. I never did let her take me on that spending spree. "I don't know," I answered, knowing she'd bug me for saving it.

"I don't know what I did with my share either. Just spent it on this and that."

Things weren't that bad at the group home. In fact, it was pretty quiet until one night in the middle of July. We were all sitting in the living room, watching a really bad science-fiction movie about psychic aliens who read your mind and then sucked your brain out. There was a loud explosion in the backyard. Darren led the charge as we all ran outside. Brian was lying flat out in the middle of the yard, unconscious. His face was a horrible red, and his clothes were burned and blackened. There were scraps of metal around the yard and a small fire in the grass where something had exploded.

"Call 9-1-1!" Darren shouted, and I flipped open my old phone and punched in the numbers. When asked what the emergency was, I had a hard time explaining. But I guess I said enough to get an ambulance headed our way.

Connor started walking around the yard in circles, ranting. "Brian, you freaking idiot," he said. "You could have killed us all. You dumb, stupid piece of shit."

This really pissed off Kyle, who I had never seen really angry before. Kyle said, "Shut up, Connor. Just shut up," and then Kyle kicked him hard in the ass, making Connor slam forward into the high wooden fence.

Darren started CPR on Brian and told Noah to go watch for the ambulance and wave it down. "What can I do?" I asked.

"Pray," Darren said. I didn't know if he meant it, but I tried. I wasn't at all sure I believed in God, but I silently asked for Brian not to die. I felt helpless standing there, but a strange feeling came over me. It was like someone had heard my request. There was a voice in my head, the voice of my mother, telling me everything would be okay. Looking at Brian, it didn't seem that way at all.

When the paramedics arrived, Darren went with Brian to the hospital. He didn't get back until late that night. Connor was sulking in his room. Noah, Kyle and I were sitting in the kitchen.

"He's gonna be okay," Darren said. "The burns are bad, but they'll heal. But it's not going to be pretty." He looked at the three of us. "Can anyone tell me what he was up to?"

"He was making a bomb," Kyle said. Kyle roomed with Brian. "Some kind of homemade bomb he found out about on the Internet. I thought it was just talk, but I guess he figured out how to do it. I'm sorry. I should have said something."

Darren looked at Kyle and then at Noah and me. "No secrets," he said. "Let's keep it all out in the open. Even if you think you are ratting on someone." I couldn't tell if he was mad at us for some reason or mad at himself for letting something like this happen. He ran his hand through his hair. It was the first time I'd seen Darren when he didn't seem to have it all together. "Do you think he was hoping to blow us all up?" he asked no one in particular.

"No," Kyle said. "He likes it here. Sort of. He said that. He had this thing about wanting to do something, um, dangerous. I thought it was just an act."

Darren shook his head. Then he got up and looked around the kitchen. We were all a bit shocked when he clenched his fist like he was going to hit something. Instead, he kicked over a chair and walked out of the room.

Things were quiet around the house for a week or so after that. We visited Brian a few times at the hospital. He apologized to all of us and said he'd never do something that stupid again. Looking at his burned face, I couldn't help but think what a sorry lot we were. Each of us was damaged in some way and looking for a way to act it out. But I knew it wasn't just us. There were a lot of screwed-up people out there.

On our way back to the house, I said some of what I was thinking to Darren.

"You're so right, Josh. I don't know why it is, but you are bang on. Why don't you do something about it?"

"What do you mean?"

"You've got a life ahead of you. Why not try to heal some of that damage?" He looked at me and he was dead serious.

I almost laughed. "I have a hard enough time holding myself together. I doubt I could do much good for anyone else."

"Yes, you could. Use your own pain to do some good for others." It was the preachy Darren that I knew.

In those days after the bomb I did some serious thinking about where I was and where I was going. I thought a lot about Lindsey. I missed her even though I knew that she was trouble. If I hung out with her long enough, she'd get me involved in another one of her scams. I figured she could probably talk her way out of anything. Or she would just cry and get away with it. But not me.

I hadn't heard from her for a while, and she wasn't answering my calls. That didn't feel right. I wondered if maybe she'd lost interest in me and moved on. When she finally did answer her phone, I asked her what she'd been up to.

"I've been spending a lot of time on the Internet," she said.

"Doing what?"

"Just having some fun," she said. "Man, summer can be so boring."

"Not around here," I said, and I told her all about our recent catastrophe. But I was afraid to ask her more about what she was doing on the Internet, afraid to hear what kind of scams she was up to.

Chapter Twelve

Darren announced that he had volunteered Kyle, Noah, Connor and me to spend the next three days at a day camp not far away, working with little kids from disadvantaged homes. Connor complained that it wasn't his responsibility "to babysit impoverished rug rats," and we wasted an evening hearing him rant about it, but in the end he went along, even if he was a pain in the butt about it.

All we did was kick some balls around and play games. I'd never really spent much time with younger kids, and I was kind of shocked that they treated me like an adult and that I was actually good at keeping them occupied.

I talked to Lindsey on the phone each evening, and each time she seemed more distant. I wondered if she'd found a new guy on the Internet or maybe just lost interest or invented some new devious hobby to occupy her time. When I began to believe that I was losing her altogether, I got up my courage and asked her to meet me downtown. I said I'd buy her dinner at McDonald's.

"I'd like to, but I'm busy, Josh. I have some new friends that I'm getting together with." We talked a bit more. As I said goodbye, I felt a sharp twinge of sadness. I was pretty sure Lindsey was slipping away from me. She'd probably realized what a loser I was and was ready to move on.

I spent a couple more days at the summer camp, and I liked it even more than I had at first. Some of these kids were starved for attention. It wasn't hard to get them smiling and involved in games. I told Darren I was willing to work at the camp as long as I could.

Darren smiled. "Nice. I watched you. You're a rock star to them. Keep it up."

My calls to Lindsey went unanswered. I'd get her voice mail and leave a message, but she never called back. I guessed I was ready to close that freaky little chapter in my so-called life.

But then she called. It was about eleven thirty one night. Noah had already woken me up by shouting during one of his nightmares. In Noah's mind, his father just kept beating the crap out of him, even long after he was gone.

When I answered the phone, all I heard was sobbing. I knew it was her. "Lindsey, what's wrong?" I asked.

At first she didn't answer. Just more sobbing.

"Tell me," I insisted. "What happened?"

"I'm sorry," she said. "I shouldn't have called." And she hung up.

I called her right back. At first she didn't answer. But finally she did.

"It's my brother," she said. "Caleb. He fell. He was way up on the side of an abandoned warehouse."

"Is he okay?"

There was a long pause. I heard Lindsey sucking in a breath. "No. He's dead."

I didn't know what to say. I felt frozen. I pictured a kid high up on the side of a building with a spray can of paint, leaving his silly nickname. For what? Just to say, *Look at me. I was here. Aren't I great?* It made no sense.

"Are you going to be okay?" I asked foolishly.

"No. I'm not going to be okay. I lost my brother." She now sounded like she was angry at me.

"I'm going to come over."

"No."

"Are you home?"

"Yes."

"How do I find you?"

While I was putting on my clothes, Noah woke up. I explained what had happened and where I was going. "Don't tell Darren," I said.

"No," he said. "Tell Darren."

"What if he doesn't let me go?"

"Tell Darren," he repeated.

And when I told Darren, all he said was, "I'll drive you."

There were no lectures on the way. No advice except "Do what you have to do." And as I closed the car door and walked to Lindsey's front door, I didn't have a clue what I could do to help. All I knew was that I wanted to be there for her.

It was a pretty fancy house, and there were two cars in the driveway— a Mercedes and a BMW. Lindsey must have heard the car drive up, because she opened the door. She looked like she'd been crying for a really long time.

"Where are your parents?" I asked.

"Finally asleep, thank God. The police came to tell us. It was horrible. When they left, my mom was crying and my dad started blaming her for this. Then she tore into him. They'd been drinking. I just shut myself in my room. That's when I called you."

"Why me?" I asked.

"I don't know. I just knew you were the one I needed to talk to."

I wrapped my arms around her and held her close. "Stay with me," she said. "Don't leave."

She led me up to her bedroom, and she threw herself down on top of her bed. I cautiously lay down beside her. A little lamp was on, and there was a soft glow in the room. I lay on my back with her beside me and she cried a bit more, and then I held her until she fell asleep. I didn't fall asleep that night. I just listened to her breathe—ragged at first, and then slower and more steady.

What happens next? I kept asking myself as I lay there. What do I do?

But there were no answers.

Chapter Thirteen

I awoke to a knock on the door.

"Lindsey," a male voice said. "Your mother and I have to go deal with this. Will you be okay?"

Lindsey sat upright and saw me lying there on top of the bed. She cleared her throat. "Yeah, Dad. You go do what you have to do."

Then a woman's voice said, "Lindsey, are you sure you're okay? Can I come in?"

"No, Mom. Really. I'm okay. Don't come in. I just want to be left alone right now. I just want to sleep."

"Okay," she said. And I heard their footsteps on the stairs, and then the front door opened and closed.

I sat up beside Lindsey and looked around her room. It seemed odd that it was filled with so many little-girl kind of things—dolls, stuffed animals and photos of her when she was younger.

I was still blinking the sleep out of my eyes when she leaned into me and began to cry again. "I can't believe he's gone. This can't be happening," she said. "I just want to go somewhere and hide."

"Were you two close?"

"We used to be. When we were young we did a lot of things together. Bike riding, swimming, skateboarding."

"Somehow I can't picture you on a skateboard."

"I was awesome," she said, trying to smile, but the smile gave way to a new wave of sadness.

"I bet you were."

"But we were bad too."

"I can believe that," I said.

"We put our parents through hell." She looked at me long and hard. "And now this."

"Yeah, this." I hugged her to me and couldn't help but think about my own loss.

"Caleb wasn't much good at any particular thing until he got into the graffiti. I mean, he was always trying too hard to be like someone else. Always trying to be good at sports when he wasn't. Trying to be tough when it wasn't his nature. Trying to win over girls when they didn't want anything to do with him. He would get depressed.

Really depressed. For days at a time. And I'd try to snap him out of it.

"And then he decided he wanted to be an artist, and he ended up with spray cans of paint. Most people would think of it as vandalism, but it was his thing. He was proud of what he did. Kids admired him for it. The crazy dangerous and difficult places where his work would show up. And he never got caught. Not once. But he didn't deserve this."

"No, he didn't. I wish I could have gotten to know him."

"Thanks for saying that."

We sat in the kitchen and drank coffee. There was mostly silence between us now. I was wishing I could do more, say the right things, but I knew from my own experience that it didn't matter much what people said to you. The pain didn't go away. After a while Lindsey's cell phone beeped. She had a text.

She read it and then pounded back some message, with an angry look on her face.

"What?" I asked after she slammed the phone down on the table.

"They're at a funeral home. They want me to get a cab and meet them there. I said no way."

By midmorning she said she just wanted to go back to bed and sleep. "It would be better if you weren't here when my parents get home."

I didn't ask why, but I didn't want to complicate things. I kissed Lindsey on the forehead and held her hands. "Just let me know what I can do," I said. "I'll do anything to help." And I meant it.

She didn't answer her phone or return my calls again for two days. I talked to Darren for some advice.

"When people grieve, they tend to shut others out of their lives. Sounds like she had already shut her parents out.

And that's not good. But keep at it. Don't give up."

I'd been holding back, giving her space, but after that I figured I better do something. I went back to her house and rang the doorbell. Her mother answered.

"Can I see Lindsey?"

"She isn't here. Who are you?"

"Josh. I'm a friend."

"She never mentioned you." I knew Lindsey didn't communicate much of anything to her parents, so it didn't surprise me that she hadn't mentioned me.

"I know about Caleb," I said. "I wanted to see if I can help."

Lindsey's mom looked me in the eye with suspicion, but then she looked down and let out a sigh. "You could help find Lindsey. We haven't seen her since…" But she didn't finish the sentence.

"She hasn't been home?"

"No. We're very worried." Now Lindsey's mom started to cry.

"I'll find her," I said. "I promise." And I turned to go.

Lindsey's mom grabbed my sleeve and pulled me back. "The funeral is tomorrow. It would be a terrible thing if she wasn't there."

"I'll find her," I repeated.

Chapter Fourteen

I walked downtown and went to the coffee shop where we had once sat. I asked the people working there if they'd seen her, but no one had. I wished I had a picture of her to show them, but I didn't. The thought made me open my wallet and look at that old beat-up photo of my mom. I looked at it and silently asked her what to do. I could swear I heard her tell me to keep looking.

Lindsey was smart, and she was resourceful. And she was also stubborn. If she really wanted to make herself disappear, she would find a way to do it. But this wasn't one of her scams. This was real life.

I walked the streets for hours. There were a lot of tourists out and about. Lindsey would have had a field day with this. Easy pickings. I went to the park. I went to the church hall where we had stolen the wedding cards. I talked to any kids our age that I saw. I came up with nothing.

I felt like all I could do was make the same rounds again. It seemed hopeless. Was she just going to disappear from my life as mysteriously as she had come into it? *Damn*. I was sitting on a crumbling low wall by the library when

I looked up and realized I was across the street from the church where we had first sat together at my mother's funeral.

It seemed like the least likely place to find her. But I was desperate. I walked across the street and tried the door. It was unlocked. I went in. The place was completely empty. At first I hated being there. The pain of it all. That stupid ceremony for my mom with all those strangers. But as I walked forward down the aisle, I looked up and saw light pouring in through the stained-glass windows. There was something about that light. Something that made me keep walking toward the front.

And then I saw her. Lying in a pew. Curled up in the fetal position.

I slipped into the pew and quietly sat down beside her. I sat like that for maybe five minutes—watching her sleep, watching her breathe, realizing how important this girl was to me.

And then I touched her shoulder. She gasped, sat up, looked at me. And then she reached up and hugged me.

When we walked out into the sunlight, we both had to shield our eyes. We hadn't even spoken a word.

"Your mom says the funeral is tomorrow," I said.

"I'm not going," she said resolutely.

"I understand," I said. "But you should be there for your parents."

"Screw them. My parents were never there for me when I needed them."

"But they're still your parents," I said, knowing that sounded lame. "You should at least go home. Let them see you're okay."

"I'm not going home."

"Then come with me," I said.

As we walked to the group home, we went past the old warehouse wall that Caleb had tagged. I tried to distract Lindsey so she wouldn't see the balloon letters of *Yo-Yo*, but she stopped, stared up at the name for a minute and then looked away. I took her hand.

Darren must have seen us walking up the driveway. In an instant, he must have read the riot act to Kyle, Noah and Connor, because they were all sitting in a kind of stunned silence in the kitchen as we walked in.

"You must be Lindsey," Darren said.

She nodded.

"You need a place to stay?"

She nodded again.

"Why don't you take over Josh's room?" Darren said. "Noah can bunk with Connor, and I'm sure Josh wouldn't mind sleeping on the sofa."

Connor glared at Noah, but he didn't say a word. Noah nodded agreeably, but Kyle looked a little shell-shocked that I had brought a girl to the house.

Lindsey and I sat in the backyard for a long time, but we didn't say much.

I thought maybe she was settling down, but I was wrong. "Everything about being around this town is just too painful. I mean, you saw me back there. I'm not gonna be able to go hardly anywhere without my brother calling out to me from some wall. I've got some money. I could just pick up and go. Go somewhere else and put this all behind me."

I had a lot of things I wanted to say, but I was afraid of saying the wrong thing. I had her here now. I wouldn't say too much, but I wouldn't let her slip away.

Later, I asked her if it was okay for me to call her parents and let them know she was all right. She said no, but after I pushed, she agreed that I could call them as long as I didn't let them know where she was. Just that she was okay. I called and was relieved when I got their voice mail. I told them Lindsey was okay and would call the next day. In the evening my roommates were quiet and respectful, even Connor. Whatever threat Darren had made must have been a good one.

I got up about twenty times from the sofa in the living room during the night to make sure she was still in my room. In the morning everyone else left the house to go work at the summer day camp. Lindsey and I sat alone in the kitchen, drinking some truly awful coffee that Darren had made. Today was the day of Caleb's funeral. I didn't know the time or the place. But today was the day.

"You saved me that day, you know?" I said.

"What day?"

"The day you stole my wallet."

"How did that save you?"

"Well, if you hadn't stolen my wallet, I wouldn't have run after you.

And you wouldn't have gone to the church with me."

"What would you have done?"

"I don't know. Like you, I was thinking about maybe just going away."

"Where?"

"Anywhere."

"So you understand?"

"Yes. But I also understand that I owe you."

"How?" she asked.

"It won't work. If you go away, everything back here will seem like crap to you. You won't be able to let it go, and you won't be able to put it behind you. It will always be there. It will always be unfinished. And you'll be unhappy."

"Bullshit."

"No. No bullshit. It's true. Today is the funeral. One phone call, and I'll know where and when."

"No way," she said.

"Do you care about me at all?"

"Yes."

"Do you trust me?"

"I guess."

"Then trust me on this. Do this one thing. If you decide it's wrong, that I've somehow betrayed you, I'll go away too if you want. We'll go together."

Lindsey stared down at the table for a solid minute. "Find out where it is and what time," she said. "Then I'll decide. But don't tell them I will necessarily be there."

We arrived at the funeral home ten minutes after the service had begun. A minister was reading from the bible. Unlike my mom's service, there was a casket at the front, and it was open. The chapel was maybe half full. We walked up the aisle. I watched as Lindsey's mom and dad turned and saw us as we were sitting down. Her mom closed her eyes and squeezed her hands together in front of her face. Lindsey sat staring at the casket in the front. I don't think she was expecting it to be like this. Almost as soon as she had sat down, she stood back up and began walking to the front of the chapel.

The minister stopped reading as he noticed her approaching. The chapel was dead silent. I held back. I wondered if I had it all wrong. Maybe I shouldn't have brought her here. She slowly approached the casket, leaned over. She kissed her brother on the forehead and then took his hand. Some of the people in the chapel began to weep. No one moved. And then her parents got up and walked forward to stand beside her.

Chapter Fifteen

Lindsey and I both began our final year of high school that September. Because I was living at the group home, I got transferred to a new high school, the same one Lindsey went to.

I can't quite explain what happened next. We had been with each other almost every day for the rest of that summer. She'd helped me at that day camp. She'd liked the kids, and they had liked her.

One day we even came across one of the twelve-year-old boys from the camp while we were downtown. The kid's name was Duke—at least, that was his nickname. Duke saw us walking down the street and came up to us. "Josh, can you spot me some money? My mom gave me bus fare, but I lost it. I can't get home if I don't have bus fare."

Lindsey leaned over. "Did you really lose your money?"

"Yeah, of course I did," the kid said. "Would I lie to you?"

Everyone at summer camp knew Duke was a little scam artist. He wasn't that good at it, really, but then, he was just starting out.

Lindsey held out a five-dollar bill. "You can have it if you tell me the truth."

Duke blinked and looked at her. "Truth is, I want to go to McDonald's and get a snack."

Lindsey almost handed him the money then but pulled it back. "Promise you won't try to con anyone again?" she said.

"Maybe," he said. And she gave him the money.

It had been a sad summer for us both. But we moved on.

And that was part of the problem. We moved on. Both of us. By the end of September, Lindsey had fallen back in with some old friends from the previous year. I don't know if they didn't like me or if maybe they just didn't know what to make of me. I had decided to really try hard and do well at school that year, and with a little help from Darren, it was working out. And then Lindsey and I just drifted apart. We both tried to keep what we had, but something had changed that we could not change back. Each time we were together, it seemed we both felt the pain of our losses creep up on us, and we'd fall silent.

I guess it can happen like that. It's sad but true. I still feel bad that what we had is gone. All I know is that while we were together, it was real. Very real.

Lesley Choyce has written many books for Orca, including the recent *Off the Grid*. A poet, author and publisher, Lesley is also an avid surfer. He lives in Nova Scotia.